This book is to be returned on or before
the last date

...BERT B. PARKER

Level 3

Retold by Robin Waterfield
Series Editors: Andy Hopkins and Jocelyn Potter

Pearson Education Limited
Edinburgh Gate, Harlow,
Essex CM20 2JE, England
and Associated Companies throughout the world.

ISBN 0 582 41681 7

A Catskill Eagle copyright © Robert B. Parker 1985
First published in Great Britain by Viking 1986
Published in Penguin Books 1986
This adaptation first published by Penguin Books 1994
Published by Addison Wesley Longman Limited and Penguin Books Ltd. 1998
New edition first published 1999

Text copyright © Robin Waterfield 1994
Illustrations copyright © Bob Harvey 1994
All rights reserved

The moral right of the adapter and of the illustrator has been asserted

Typeset by RefineCatch Limited, Bungay, Suffolk
Set in 11/14pt Monotype Bembo
Printed in Spain by Mateu Cromo, S.A. Pinto (Madrid)

Published by Pearson Education Limited in association with
Penguin Books Ltd., both companies being subsidiaries of Pearson Plc

For a complete list of the titles available in the Penguin Readers series please write to your local
Pearson Education office or to: Marketing Department, Penguin Longman Publishing,
5 Bentinck Street, London W1M 5RN.

Contents

Introduction

'Costigan wants you dead,' Quirk said. 'He has ordered his men to find and kill you. If you don't kill him, he'll kill you sooner or later.'

Boston detective, Spenser, makes enemies – a lot of enemies. That's because he plays by *his* rules, not other people's. When his friend Hawk wrongly goes to prison, Spenser gets him out – with a gun.

Now the police want him – but Jerry Costigan wants him too. And Costigan is much more dangerous than the police. Costigan put Hawk in prison in the first place. Now he'll kill Hawk *and* Spenser if he can.

But there are other people in this game, people who want to stop Costigan. They don't play by other people's rules, either – they don't play by *any* rules. And if Spenser helps them, *they'll* help him . . .

Robert B. Parker was born in 1932 in Massachusetts. He studied English in Waterville, Maine, from 1950 to 1954, then went to Korea with the United States army for two years. After he returned to America, he worked as a writer in business, but hated the work. He wanted a job that gave him time for writing, but also enough money for his family. So in 1962 he left business and studied to become a university teacher.

He wanted to write like Raymond Chandler, one of the greatest of all American detective writers, but it was nine years before he had time to write his first book, *The Godwulf Manuscript*. He was forty-one years old when it came out in 1974. He left teaching in 1979, and has written many more books. Most of them are about his detective, Spenser. All his books are best-sellers, and there are now Spenser films and TV programmes.

Chapter 1   A Letter from Susan

It was nearly midnight and I was just getting home from work. I work as a detective. I took a bottle of beer from the fridge, opened it and sat down to read my post. There was a letter from Susan. The letter said:

I have no time. Hawk is in prison in Mill River, California. You must get him out. I need help too. Hawk will explain. Things are terrible, but I love you.

Susan

I read the letter again. The words were still the same; the meaning was still the same. It seemed to me that Susan was frightened. The letter came from San Jose.

I drank some beer. Then I went to the phone. My lawyer Vince Haller answered after thirty seconds.

'It's Spenser,' I said.

He said, 'It's the middle of the night. I was asleep.'

I said, 'Hawk's in prison in a small town called Mill River, south of San Francisco. I want you to get a lawyer in there now.'

'In the middle of the night?'

'It's not the middle of the night *there*, in California. It's only the middle of the night here in Boston,' I replied.

'What kind of trouble is Hawk in?' Vince asked.

'I don't know. Hawk knows. Get a lawyer down there now.'

'OK. I know someone out there. She'll go and see. Wait for her to call you.'

'OK. But hurry, please, Vince.'

I got another beer and read Susan's letter again. It said the same thing.

◆

The phone went at three o'clock in the morning.
A woman's voice said, 'Mr Spenser?'

The phone went at three o'clock in the morning. A woman's voice said, 'Mr Spenser?'

I said yes.

She said, 'This is Paula Goldman. I'm a lawyer from San Francisco.'

'Have you seen Hawk?' I asked.

'Yes. He's in a cell in Mill River, California. The police arrested him for murder. He killed a man called Emmett Colder, who worked for a man called Russell Costigan. Hawk also hurt several policemen. It seems to be difficult to arrest him.'

'Yes,' I said.

'He agrees that he killed Colder, but he says that he was only defending himself.'

'Can you get him out?'

'Perhaps, but the problem is that Russell Costigan's father is Jerry Costigan.'

'No!'

'You know Jerry Costigan.'

'I know who he is. He owns half this country.'

'Right, and one of the things which he owns is Mill River, California,' she said. 'So there's no hope for Hawk. It doesn't matter what he did or didn't do. What matters is that he broke three of Russell Costigan's teeth. And he's black. The Costigans don't like black people.'

I was quiet for a short time, then I asked: 'Did he say anything about Susan Silverman?'

'He came to California because she asked him to, but they were waiting for him. That's all he said. The police were listening to our conversation, and I guess he didn't want to say more in front of them. The police in Mill River are friendly with Jerry Costigan, if you know what I mean.'

'So that's all you know?'

'That's all I know.'

'Tell me about the Mill River police station.'

She said, 'I'm a lawyer. I can't help a prisoner escape. It's against the law.' But she described the small-town prison perfectly. There were only four cells in the Mill River police station.

Chapter 2   Mill River

Before I left Boston, a friend made a cast for my leg. It was too big, so I could put it on and take it off easily. When I was wearing it, I seemed to have a broken leg. I put dirt on the cast so that it looked old and used. It lay at the bottom of my bag while I flew to San Francisco and then drove through San Jose to Mill River.

I found the police station. Opposite the police station there was a library. I parked in the carpark behind the library and got the cast out of my bag. Inside the cast, there was a place where I could hide a small gun. I hid my gun there, took off my shoe and put the cast on. I got out of the car and hid the keys in the carpark.

I bought a bottle of cheap wine from a supermarket and put some on my clothes. I smelled bad and had a two-day beard. I sat outside the library with the bottle in my hand and said rude things to the people walking past. Before long two policemen arrested me and took me to the police station.

They took me past the cell where Hawk was. He was lying on the bed, his hands behind his head.

'Hey, black boy!' I shouted.

Hawk opened his eyes and looked at me. His eyes showed nothing. 'Yeah, whitey? You talkin' to me?'

*I sat outside the library with the bottle in my hand and
said rude things to the people walking past.*

'Stop that!' said one of the policemen. They locked me in my cell. There was nothing for me to do for hours, so I slept.

◆

'What's happening in here?' asked the young policeman.

It was two in the morning, and Hawk and I were making a lot of noise.

'I'm singing the black man to sleep,' I said. I hit my shoe against the wall of the cell in time with the song which I was singing.

'Hey, Maury, get in here,' called the young policeman.

A second policeman arrived. I continued singing. Hawk was silent. The young one pulled a switch and my cell door opened. Both the policemen came in. 'We're going to teach you to be quiet,' the older one said.

I pulled the gun out from under my shirt and pointed it at them. 'If you make any noise,' I said, 'I'll kill you.'

Both of them stopped and stayed where they were.

I took their guns from them. 'Are you the only ones in the building?' I asked.

'No, there's Madilyn on the phones,' Maury answered.

I left the cell and went over to the switches on the wall. I locked the cell which the policemen were in, and opened the one which Hawk was in. He came out and walked over to me. I gave him one of the guns.

' "Black boy", huh?' he said.

'Get Madilyn,' I said.

We locked Madilyn in Hawk's cell, and left the police station. I got the car keys and we drove towards San Jose. 'They'll come after us soon,' Hawk said. 'As soon as one of the police cars returns to the station.'

'We have to go to Susan's place,' I said.

'They'll look there first,' Hawk said.

We locked Madilyn in Hawk's cell, and left the police station.

'I know,' I said.

But there was nobody there. I looked in the bathroom and bedroom cupboards, and said to Hawk, 'She's left town.'

We climbed out of a back window at the same time that the police were arriving at the front of the building. We drove north to San Francisco.

Chapter 3   Russell Costigan

It was a clear night with a lot of stars. I asked Hawk to tell me about Susan.

'Some of this is going to hurt,' said Hawk.

'I know,' I said.

'Last year,' said Hawk, 'while she was still in Boston, Susan met Russell Costigan and he offered her a job in Mill River at the Costigan Hospital.'

'One of the family businesses,' I said.

'Yeah. So when you and Susan started having your troubles, she remembered Costigan and spoke to him again. She came out here. Before long, she and Costigan . . .' Hawk looked at me carefully.

'Go on,' I said.

'She really liked him. But she was still writing to you, and talking to you on the phone and everything. She doesn't want to lose you, but at the same time she's with Costigan. Costigan doesn't understand. He wants her to live with him, but she doesn't want to. "How can you love both of us at the same time?" he asks. Susan doesn't know, and she's breaking in two. She can't go back to you and leave Costigan, but she still wants you. She started to pull back from Costigan, and Costigan didn't like that. He was coming to her house when she asked him not to, and things like that. I said, "Why don't you come back east with me? Spenser and I will make it better. There's nothing we can't make better." She started to cry. Just then, Costigan comes in, and he's got two men with him.'

'Only two?' I asked.

'And Susan said, "Russell, what are you doing?" But Russell just looked at me and told me to leave. He called me some rude names and I hit him in the mouth. The two men came over and wanted to play as well. I hit one of them with a chair and he died.'

'And the police came,' I said.

'Yeah. About ten of them, with guns.'

'No one called them. They were waiting.'

'That's right. I think they listened to Susan on the phone when she called me.'

'Who listened?' I asked. 'The police or Costigan?'

'It doesn't matter,' Hawk said. 'Costigan owns the police.'

We were silent for a few minutes. Then I said, 'You broke three of Costigan's teeth.'

'I left plenty more for you,' Hawk said.

'I know. We'll get to that. But first we find Susan.'

Chapter 4 Transpan

We found a safe place to stay in San Francisco. 'Now what?' asked Hawk.

'I don't know,' I said. 'We don't know where Susan is, and we don't know much about the Costigans. So I think I'll phone Rachel Wallace.'

'Who's she?' asked Hawk.

'Rachel Wallace is a writer that I know in New York. She's good at getting information out of libraries. We can't do it, because we have to stay off the streets.'

On the TV news, we saw that the police were searching
everywhere for Hawk and me.

Rachel was happy to help. On the TV news, we saw that the police were searching everywhere for Hawk and me.

'Everywhere?' said Hawk.

'Nearly everywhere,' I said.

'They're probably looking for a handsome black man and an ugly white man,' said Hawk.

'We're perfectly safe, then,' I said.

◆

Hawk and I waited. We didn't want to go outside because the news programmes were showing our faces on TV.

'It's hard doing nothing,' Hawk said. 'If we have to stay here one more day, watching daytime TV, I'll call the police and tell them where we are.'

'Waiting is doing something,' I said.

'It's hard waiting,' he said. 'It's hard not to think while you're waiting.'

'I'm thinking about how to find her,' I said. 'That's all.'

Hawk didn't seem sure that this was quite true.

Rachel Wallace phoned in the early evening.

'Jerry Costigan lives in a big house in Mill River,' she said, 'but he has other houses all over the country. He is very, very rich. After his father died, he built a small local business into one of the biggest businesses in America. The name of the business is Transpan. He carries things by road and by aeroplane, not just coast to coast, but to other countries as well. He owns hotels, farms and TV stations; he puts money into films and pop musicians. But mostly he makes weapons. Jerry owns Transpan, but Russell – who is his only child – is the boss of some of the smaller businesses. They have offices in most cities.'

'Interesting,' I said. 'Any more?'

'Jerry's wife's name is Grace; they married in 1944. Russell

11

was born in 1945. In 1970, he married a woman called Tyler Smithson. They have two children. The wife and the children live in Chicago.' She gave me the address, and then went on, 'But listen: the most important thing is that it doesn't seem to matter to the Costigans who their customers are. They sell weapons to both sides in a war; they sell to enemies of the United States. Jerry nearly got into trouble with the government for doing that once, in the 1950s. And it's possible that they also send men to countries at war. First they sell them the weapons, then they send in men to teach them to use the weapons. That's all I can tell you.'

'Thanks, Rachel,' I said.

'I'll phone you if I have more information for you,' she said.

♦

I told Hawk everything. 'We still don't know where Susan is,' he said. 'These Costigans have places all over the country. They know we're looking for her. You can be sure that Russell has taken her somewhere safe by now.'

'I know,' I said. 'I don't know what to do. She won't be at the house in Mill River.'

'Where do you think she'll be, then?'

'I don't know. Anywhere.'

'Also,' Hawk went on, 'we need more weapons. Russell is not going to just give her to you. He's got men. He's going to defend himself, and her.'

'Yeah, I know. We need money too,' I said, 'and a car. We have to go back to Boston to get all these things. We're sure she's not here, so let's go.'

The Costigans sell weapons to enemies of the United States. Jerry
nearly got into trouble with the government for doing that once.

Chapter 5   A Job for Spenser

It was dangerous to go back to our places in Boston, so we stayed in the empty flat of one of Hawk's friends. When I phoned my telephone answering machine, I found that Lieutenant Quirk of the Boston police wanted to speak to me. I also found that Jerry Costigan wanted to kill me. He was kind enough to phone me and tell me. 'Spenser, you're a dead man,' he said. 'No one tries to hurt my son and lives.'

I told Hawk. 'Quirk's a good man,' Hawk said. 'He won't just arrest you. Phone him, and we'll meet.'

I called Quirk. In about ten seconds he came to the phone.

'Spenser,' I said.

'I know that name,' Quirk said. 'The Californian police want to arrest you for breaking every law in the book.'

'It was nothing,' I said. 'Hawk helped too.'

'I want to talk,' Quirk said. 'Be on the corner of Charles and Chestnut at nine.'

At 9:02 a brown Chevrolet stopped at the corner of Charles and Chestnut. Sergeant Belson was driving. Quirk sat next to him. Hawk and I got into the back and Belson drove back into the traffic, towards the Common. Quirk turned and looked at us.

'You've been busy,' he said. 'Why did you do all those things?'

'Susan's in trouble,' I said.

'She's not the only one,' said Belson.

Quirk thought for a moment. 'We're going to go and meet two men,' he said. 'One works for the FBI and the other for the CIA. They want to talk to you.'

'What about?' I asked.

'They want to talk about helping you with the Californian police.'

'We're going to go and meet two men,' Quirk said.
'One works for the FBI and the other for the CIA.'

'That's good of them,' said Hawk.

'Yeah,' I said. 'Isn't that nice?'

'And then maybe you can help them with something,' Quirk said.

'Of course,' I said.

'They want you to kill Costigan,' Quirk said.

Belson took his dead cigar out of his mouth and threw it out of the car window. He took another one out of his pocket and lit it. It smelled like a burning shoe.

'We'll be pleased to help our government,' Hawk said.

'Oh, yes,' I agreed.

Belson stopped at a restaurant in Watertown. He stayed in the car while the rest of us went inside. Two men were sitting at a table at the back of the restaurant. It was sunny and warm, but both men were wearing raincoats.

No one said anything while the waitress brought us our coffees. Then McKinnon said, 'McKinnon, FBI. This is Ives.'

Ives said, 'There are three letters after my name.'

'He's with the CIA,' Quirk explained.

When Quirk said the secret letters, Ives looked uncomfortable. 'Let's not tell everyone in the world, Lieutenant,' he said.

Hawk looked round the empty restaurant and said, 'What?' Quirk tried to hide a smile.

'All right, all right,' McKinnon said. 'We know you two are real funny. Now let's do some business.'

'We're trying to do this in a friendly way,' Ives said. 'We don't have to. I can order Lieutenant Quirk to arrest you and then we can talk, if you like.'

Quirk looked carefully at Ives and spoke very clearly. 'You can't order Lieutenant Quirk to do anything, Ives. All you can do is ask.'

Ives cleared his throat. 'Let's begin again,' he said. 'I think you can help us, and we can help you.'

'We're listening,' I said.

'You probably know,' Ives went on, 'that Costigan sells weapons. There's nothing wrong with that, usually, but Costigan secretly sells weapons to countries the government doesn't want him to sell to. That's against the law.'

He waited while the waitress came and put the bill down in front of McKinnon. Then Ives continued.

'We – the government – have had several men inside Costigan's business, but each time these men have disappeared. But we've heard that he wants his weapons business to grow. He's going to start buying and selling not just more weapons, but much larger and more dangerous ones. Some governments in the world just aren't sensible, and these are the kinds of weapons no one wants to see in their hands. We wanted to find a way to stop Costigan, and then we learned that you two want to get him too.'

Hawk said, 'It doesn't matter to me if Cosrigan is alive or dead; it doesn't matter to me who he sells weapons to. What matters to me is getting Susan back.'

I agreed and said, 'It's only Russell Costigan that I want.'

'It's the same thing,' McKinnon said. 'You know and I know that Russell is hiding behind his father. If you get the father, you get Russell, if you want, and the girl.'

'Woman,' I said. 'But I'm not sure she's a prisoner.'

'And Jerry Costigan is real bad,' Ives said. 'We're talking about saving thousands of lives around the world. Our information tells us that you two are the people who can do it.'

'Costigan wants you dead,' Quirk said. 'He has ordered his men to find and kill you – both of you. If you don't kill him, he'll kill you sooner or later.'

17

'And if we do it,' I said, 'you'll get the Californian police to forget all about us?'

'That's right,' Ives said. 'But you have to kill Costigan. If your girlfriend just walks away from Russell and back to you, you're still in trouble with the Californian police.'

'We understand,' I said. 'We'll need a safe house, money and guns.'

'OK. We'll give you everything you want,' Ives said.

Chapter 6   Tyler Smithson

They put us in a flat on Main Street in Charlestown. In two days, Ives came back with another man who looked like a pop star. They gave us new clothes, cars, money and weapons.

'All right,' said Ives. 'Now let's look at the papers.'

We all sat round a table and the pop star showed us pictures of Jerry and Russell Costigan. They both looked like ordinary people. Then he tried to show us pictures of some of Jerry Costigan's customers.

'No,' I said.

'No?'

'No. It doesn't matter to me who Costigan's customers are. What I need is information about where they're hiding Susan Silverman.'

'Susan Silverman,' repeated the pop star, looking at Ives.

'Is this too hard for you to understand?' I said.

'The girl,' Ives said. 'She's an important part of this.'

'She's *all* of this,' I said. Hawk agreed.

'Of course,' Ives said.

The pop star looked surprised. 'They don't need to see everything?'

'Probably not,' said Ives.

Ives came back with another man who looked like a pop star.
They gave us new clothes, cars, money and weapons.

'Where's Susan? That's all we need to know,' I said. 'Can you tell us which towns Russell likes to stay in. Which flats or houses or hotels?'

'He lives with his parents in Mill Valley, north of San Francisco,' the pop star said.

Hawk turned from the window, where he was standing. He was smiling, his eyes bright. 'Mill *Valley*?' he said.

'It's good to know they're defending the country,' I said. I turned to Ives and the pop star. 'It's Mill River,' I said, 'and it's south of San Francisco.'

There was nothing more they could tell us, so they soon left. They promised to tell us anything that they learned about where Susan and Russell were. Hawk and I were not hopeful.

'We don't know where to look,' I said, 'so Chicago seems as good a place to start as any. I'll go and talk to Russell's wife, Tyler Smithson.'

◆

Tyler Smithson's flat was near the lake. The late-afternoon sun was bright and beautiful on the water. The doorman of her building phoned up to her flat and told her, 'There's a man here by the name of Spenser. He says he's come about Mr Russell Costigan.' She told him to send me up. She lived at the top of the building.

'Hello,' I said when she opened the door. She was tall and thin, with fair hair. She wore expensive clothes.

'Mr Spenser?'

'Yes.'

'Come in. Sit down. Would you like some coffee?'

'Yes, please,' I said. 'Black.'

A woman called Eunice made us both coffee. We waited for her to bring it, then Tyler Smithson asked me, 'What is it about Russell Costigan?'

She was tall and thin, with fair hair. She wore expensive clothes.

I can't think of an easy way to say this, Mrs Costigan. Russell is somewhere with a woman I love. I want to find them.'

Tyler Smithson's polite smile disappeared. 'You mean Susan? That dirty . . .'

I stayed calm. 'Yes. Can you help me find them? I'm sure we both want them to stop. I think Susan already wants to leave, and Russell is stopping her. If I find them, I'll help her to leave.'

'I don't think she wants to leave, Spenser. All his women love him. He's funny, and good to be with, and very, very rich. He gives them a good time, and then he gets bored with them. He kicks them out of his house and then comes home.'

'And you take him back?'

'The Costigans own everything they want to own. Their men watch this house, for example. They'll know you were here.'

'Yes,' I said.

'If you continue trying to find Russell, Jerry will kill you.'

'He'll try. But I'm good at what I do, Mrs Costigan. Jerry will get hurt.'

'Russell will like that. He likes to see his father lose. The boss of the family is really the mother, Grace. Russell loves her, and wants her to love him. He thinks that if his father seems smaller to her, he'll seem bigger. He probably likes your Susan partly because she's Jewish.'

'And his father doesn't like Jews,' I said.

'Nor blacks,' she said.

'If you help me,' I said, 'I'll try not to hurt him. Where do you think he and Susan are?'

'You really think you can win, don't you?'

'Yes.'

'And you think if you can get her away from Russell, she'll come back to you?'

'I'll get her away from Russell because she doesn't want to be with him. When I've done that, we'll see what she chooses to do.'

'But you want her back.'

'Yes.'

'Because you love her.'

'Yes.'

Tyler Costigan laughed, but it was a dry, unreal laugh. 'I understand that perfectly,' she said. She turned to look out of the window into the bright afternoon. 'I've got Russell and she's got you. Why is love so hard?'

She was silent for a short time, thinking. Then she said, 'They have a weapons factory in a small town in Connecticut called Pequod. That's probably where they are. It's not only a factory – it's also where they train men to fight and to use the weapons, so there are always a lot of men there. It's very safe.'

♦

As I came out of Tyler Costigan's building, a black four-door Pontiac stopped next to me. Two men got out, one from the front and one from the back. The driver stayed in the car. Both the men were very big. One was wearing a suit and the other was wearing jeans and a jacket. I could see the front of a grey Plymouth on the corner behind them, two buildings away.

The man in the suit said, 'Get in the car. We want to talk to you.' The other man stood to my left. His jacket was open.

'Are you from Costigan?' I said.

'Maybe,' the man in the suit said.

'What do you want to talk to me about?' I asked.

'About making trouble,' he said, and he opened his coat so that I could see the gun which he was wearing.

'Show me that again,' I said.

23

He opened his coat again and I hit him hard in the stomach. He fell to the ground.

He opened his coat again and I hit him hard in the stomach. He fell to the ground. The other man had his hand under his jacket, trying to get his gun, when I hit him on the nose. Blood came immediately. He nearly had his gun out. I held his wrist so that I could keep the hand with the gun under his jacket. While I was doing this, I hit him twice more on the nose and pushed him away. Out of the corner of my eye I could see the driver; he was getting out of the car on the other side. He had his gun out and was resting it on the roof of the car, pointing it at me. The grey Plymouth drove straight at him and knocked both him and the open car door down on to the road. I ran to the Plymouth and jumped in.

'Do you want me to run over the other two?' Hawk asked.

'No,' I said.

'Were they from Costigan?'

'Yes. They wanted to talk to me about making trouble.'

'Did you explain that's your job?'

'I wanted to, but he kept showing me his gun and frightening me.'

'Where shall we go now?' Hawk asked.

'Connecticut,' I said.

Chapter 7   The Weapons Factory

Pequod stands on the Farmington River, twenty miles west of Hartford. There was a shop, a garage, a church, a few wooden houses, and a hotel with a bar which was also a restaurant. Two miles out of town we found the weapons factory.

'It looks like a prison,' Hawk said.

'With all those walls and guards to defend it,' I said, 'we aren't going to be able to get inside easily.'

We drove slowly past the front entrance. A guard waved at us to move faster. We could see several low, grey-painted buildings. We could see men who looked like soldiers. There was a factory building over to the right, and some trees straight up the road behind the gate. The guard walked towards us. With him was a large dog, and he had a gun on his shoulder. We drove away.

We stayed at the hotel in Pequod and spent our days and evenings in the bar. It was the only place in town for the men from Transpan to come. We drank with them, laughed with them and fought with them; they could see that we were strong and they thought we were their friends. 'We know about weapons,' we said. 'We've fought in wars all over the world and we're looking for jobs.'

'I'll see what I can do,' said one of them, called Red.

I phoned Ives. 'Listen carefully,' I said. 'We need to get jobs at Transpan as trainers. Two other trainers have to meet accidents, if you know what I mean, so that Hawk and I can get in there.'

About two weeks later, Red took us to meet his boss, Mr Plante.

'I hear you boys are looking for work,' Plante said.

'That's right,' I said.

'We have an opening for two weapons trainers. Are you interested?'

'Sure,' I said.

'OK,' Plante said. He looked at a tall Mexican. The Mexican brought out a long knife from behind his back. 'Take the knife away from Chico,' said Plante.

Chico smiled and walked slowly and carefully towards me. When he was near, I kicked him between the legs. He dropped the knife and fell to the ground. I picked up the knife and gave it to Plante.

The guard walked towards us. With him was a large dog,
and he had a gun on his shoulder. We drove away.

'Can we have the jobs?' I asked.

'He wasn't ready,' said Plante.

'It's important to be ready all the time,' I said.

'Is he as good as you?' Plante asked, looking at Hawk.

'Maybe better,' I said.

'You can have the jobs,' he said.

◆

The work was easy. We trained the men for two hours in the morning and two hours in the afternoon. Most of the men already knew how to fight, but we had to train them so that they could go to other countries and teach others. The men that we trained came from all over the world.

Every evening we walked and looked around the place. There was a large old house behind the trees. 'Young Costigan', as Red called him, was staying there.

'He came about four weeks ago,' Red told us, 'in the middle of the night. There was a woman with him, but he often comes here with women.' Red laughed and I wanted to hit him. 'He ordered some of the men to guard the big house rather than the factory,' Red went on, 'so something important is happening.'

'Now we know where Susan is,' I said to Hawk later.

'Yeah, but how are we going to get her out?' Hawk said. 'There are too many guards, man.'

'I know,' I said. 'So near and yet so far. We'll have to wait and watch.'

Hawk began to make friends with the factory workers. The workers were all from Vietnam, though the bosses were Americans. They lived in the low, grey buildings, but in the evening they cooked on open fires outside and played cards together.

'Stay out of there,' Red told us one evening. 'Those Vietnamese will kill you for a cigarette.'

28

'Stay out of there,' Red told us one evening.
'Those Vietnamese will kill you for a cigarette.'

'Do they make trouble?' I asked.

'No,' Red said. 'The guards look after them. They broke the law coming into this country, so Transpan pays them almost nothing, shuts them away here, and they have to buy everything from the Transpan shop here. Then, when Transpan no longer needs them, the bosses kick them out and the police arrest them for coming into the country against the law.'

'Transpan owns them,' I said.

'That's right,' Red agreed.

Hawk walked over to the Vietnamese. 'Get him out of there,' Red said. 'It's dangerous in there.'

'He'll be all right,' I said.

'It's against the rules, too,' Red said.

'We can't talk to them?'

'Of course not. If people start talking to them, they'll know that Transpan is robbing them.'

Chapter 8   Sounds of Fighting

'The Vietnamese are angry,' Hawk told me a few days later.

'They weren't angry before,' I said. 'Just bored.'

'I know,' said Hawk. 'But I gave them some information that they didn't have before. They want to fight.'

'A lot of them will die,' I said.

'Yes. But most of the heavy weapons are in the weapons building. Perhaps we can stop the others getting those weapons, and give them to the Vietnamese.'

'Are they ready to go?'

'Yes,' said Hawk. 'It's hard for them to wait.'

'We can't promise them anything, but it'll be better for them to help us than to wait for Transpan to kick them out.'

'I know. I told them.'

♦

The night guard at the Transpan weapons building was a young German called Schlenker. He wore glasses when he read, and he was reading something in German with his feet up on a chair when I hit him behind the ear with the end of my gun. He fell off the chair and on to the ground.

I got the keys out of his pocket and opened the door to the gun room. Immediately, an alarm started.

Behind me, Hawk said something in Vietnamese. The Vietnamese workers came into the gun room one by one. Each took a gun and a box of bullets and left the room.

Outside, the alarm was loud and bright lights shone towards the weapons building. Hawk and I went out of a side window and heard the first gun-shots. We left the sounds of fighting behind us and went for the old house where Susan and Russell were. In front of the house, men were putting bags into a big Ford van. There were no windows in the back of the van. The men were carrying guns. They finished what they were doing. The driver got into the front, and another man got into the back of the van. Four others waited by the door of the house.

'They're leaving,' Hawk said.

Russell Costigan came out of the house, and Susan came behind him. She was wearing a black leather jacket and trousers. She looked serious, but not frightened. The guards stayed very near them while they walked to the van. There was nothing that Hawk and I could do. They got into the back of the van.

'The roof-rack,' I said. Hawk and I stood up and ran towards the van. It began to move slowly past the house. We jumped and pulled ourselves up on to the roof of the van. No

31

*Hawk held on to me while I held my gun as far out from
the side of the van as I could.*

one saw us or heard us. We lay holding the front of the roof-rack.

'Now what?' said Hawk in my ear.

'Let's hope the road is smooth,' I said.

Chapter 9   The Van

The van was travelling fast down the road. Hawk spoke into my ear again: 'We can't shoot down into the van through the roof,' he said, 'because Susan's in there.'

'No,' I said, 'but perhaps I can hit a wheel.'

Hawk held on to me while I held my gun as far out from the side of the van as I could. I pointed my gun at the back wheel and shot. Almost immediately, the van began to move from one side of the narrow country road to the other. When it was moving quite slowly, Hawk and I jumped off and hid in the darkness.

Russell climbed down on to the road and looked at the wheel too. 'Everybody out,' he said, 'while Jack changes the wheel.'

Susan took Russell's hand and he helped her out of the van.

'Leave the guns in the van,' Russell said. 'If a police car drives past, we don't want them to see the guns.'

The driver and another man, whom Russell called Curley, were starting to change the wheel when Hawk hit Curley on the head with his gun and at the same time kicked Jack in the face. Everyone turned to look at the noise, and I came up behind Russell and locked my arm around his neck. I rested my gun under his ear. Hawk was pointing his gun at the rest of the guards.

'Susan,' I said, 'walk away from the group.'

'Spenser,' she said in surprise.

I said it harder. 'Walk away.'

She did.

'The rest of you,' I said, 'lie down on the ground with your hands behind your head.'

The four guards looked at me but didn't move. Hawk shot the one who was nearest to Russell. The bullet threw him back against the van. He fell to the ground, leaving blood on the side of the van. The other guards quickly lay down on the ground with their hands behind their heads.

'You,' I said to the driver, 'finish changing the wheel.'

'I'm hurt,' he said. He was sitting on the ground with his face in his hands.

'Change it,' Hawk said softly, and the driver turned and started on the wheel.

We waited for him to finish, and then I said to Russell, 'Lie on the ground with the guards.'

'No,' he said, 'I won't lie down for you.'

'Susan, get in the van,' I said.

She didn't move.

'Suze,' I said. She went to the van and got in.

'OK,' I said. 'I'm going to drive, and Hawk's going to be looking out of the back. If any of you move, he'll shoot you.'

We drove all night, back to the safe house in Charlestown. Susan was quiet all the time.

Chapter 10   A Surprising Offer

By the next evening, after a long sleep, Susan was better. We talked for hours. 'You got my letter,' she said. 'Then what did you do?' I told her everything.

'And here we are,' I said when I finished.

'No,' he said, 'I won't lie down for you.'

'Now you have me and you haven't done anything about Jerry,' she said. 'What about that?'

'We'll still have to do something about Jerry,' I said. 'Hawk did kill a man in California, and we did escape from prison. They'll arrest us, lock us up, and throw away the key for years. So we have to do something about Jerry.'

'You have to kill Jerry Costigan or go to prison?'

'Yeah. Or he'll kill us. The trouble is that we don't know where he is.'

'What about Russell?'

'I wanted to ask you that same question,' I said.

Susan stood up and began to clean some plates and cups.

'I don't know how . . .' she began.

I waited.

'First, you understand, I love you.'

'Yes,' I said.

'But for a time you seemed to want to own me. I had to get away. Russell was different from you, and I really liked him a lot. After I called Hawk, I wanted to leave, but . . .'

'How did he stop you leaving?' I asked.

'He just said no,' she said.

'I'll gladly try to change myself, and help you to be free,' I said, 'but you can't have both of us. He goes or I go.'

'You'll leave me if I don't stop seeing Russell?'

'Yes.'

'Why didn't you kill him in Connecticut?'

'Killing him won't free you.'

'You do love me,' she said, quietly, almost to herself.

'I do. I always have,' I said.

◆

Susan was sleeping in my bedroom, and I moved in with Hawk.

36

'Does this mean you like me more than you like her?' he asked.

The days went by slowly. Susan and I had to start all over again. After a few weeks, Hawk and I were no nearer knowing where Jerry Costigan was. Ives was tired of waiting for us to kill him, but he couldn't tell us where he was either.

One day Susan said, 'I have to talk to Russell. There are things I need to say to him, to explain. If I don't, it's wrong.'

'I understand,' I said, and she went into the bedroom to make the phone call.

About ten minutes later, she came out of the room. 'He wants to talk to you,' she said.

I followed her back into the bedroom and picked up the phone. 'Yeah?' I said.

'I lost and you won with Susan,' Russell said. 'I hope you and she are lucky together, and that you're good for her. She loves me, but she loves you more. She told me.' He was trying hard to keep his voice calm. I knew how he felt. I was quiet.

'You're trying to kill my father,' he said.

'Yes.'

'He's trying to kill you.'

'Yes.'

'He's in Boise, Idaho. In an old silver mine. I'll be there too. So will my mother. It's easy to defend and he's got plenty of guards. You won't be able to get in the front; I'll show you a back way in.' He told me where to meet him.

'I'll see you there,' I said.

'Just you,' he said. 'Don't bring the black man.'

Susan was sitting on the bed, listening. 'This just gets worse and worse,' she said.

'Why is Russell doing this?' I asked.

37

'He can't lose,' she explained. 'If you die, he gets me. If his father dies, he gets his mother.'

Chapter 11   The Old Silver Mine

I met Russell on the road a few miles from the mine. We walked up a hill behind the mine. He showed me the secret way in. 'Only the family knows this passage,' he said. 'My father built it so that he could escape if there was danger. I'll see you inside.'

I went inside. It was too dark to see. I moved along the passage very carefully, touching the ground with my toes before putting each foot down. I came to some stairs and went down. My eyes were useless, so I listened hard. Nothing. I found that I could smell more. At the bottom of the stairs I smelled flowers. Flowers? What were flowers doing here, deep under the ground? Then I saw a thin line of light, shining under a door. I touched the walls until I found a switch. I pulled the switch and the door opened.

I was in the back of a cupboard. The cupboard was full of women's clothes – Mrs Costigan's, of course. I listened carefully for a long time. There was no one in the bedroom.

I walked through the bedroom, opened the door and looked out on to another passage. In a corner of the passage there was a table. A dark-haired man was sitting at the table.

I walked up to him. 'I came in last night,' I said, 'with Russell.'

'Nobody told me,' the guard said.

'You know Russell,' I said, and laughed.

'Yeah,' he said.

'Jerry wants to see me,' I said. 'Which way is it?'

He pointed. 'Second door, then down the passage,' he said. 'You'll see another guard.'

*I walked through the bedroom, opened the door and
looked out on to another passage.*

'Thanks,' I said. My mouth was dry.

I got past the second guard in the same way. He opened the door for me, and shut it behind me. In the room was a middle-aged secretary at a desk. She said, 'Can I help you?'

I said, 'Is Jerry in?'

'His family is with him,' she said warmly. 'Perhaps you can wait.'

'All right,' I said. 'But he wanted me to show you something.'

I walked over to the desk and held my left hand out in front of me, low and near the top of the desk. 'Watch,' I said, 'when I open my hand.'

She smiled and looked down. I took out my gun and hit her on the back of the head – not too hard, but hard enough. I left her with her head on the desk and went through the door into the next office. Jerry was there at his desk with his feet up, smoking a thin cigar. Grace sat in a leather chair near the wall and Russell was standing next to her.

Jerry saw the gun before he saw who held it. His face showed surprise.

Grace said, 'Jerry, do something. What does this man want?'

Russell had a strange smile on his face. Jerry looked at him.

'You showed him the way in,' he said.

'Not me,' Russell said.

'You dirty, Jew-loving pig,' Jerry said. His voice shook a little.

'Jerry,' Grace said.

Jerry looked back at me. 'Hurry up,' he said. 'Do it.'

I shot him in the heart. He turned round in his chair and lay with his shoulders and head over the side of the chair. I walked behind the desk, put my gun behind his ear and shot him once more. Then I turned towards Russell and Grace.

'We go out together,' I said. 'If I get out, you get out. If I don't, you're dead.'

'No,' Russell said. 'I won't go.'

'I shot him,' I said. 'I can shoot her too.'

'Russ,' Grace said. 'Do what he says.'

'No,' Russell said. 'He won't shoot me. He promised Susan.'

'I know you want to sit in your father's chair,' I said, 'but I'm telling you that either we all walk out of this together, or I kill you both.'

Grace said, 'Russ, you're all I've got now. Do what the man says.'

We walked past the guards, talking together in the way that old friends do. We returned to the passage behind the bedroom, but this time Grace Costigan switched on a light. I left them there. Outside on the grassy hill, the wind started to blow the darkness out of my head and my heart.

ACTIVITIES

Chapters 1–4

Before you read

1 Write down *five* words that describe a good detective. Compare your list with another student's. Which are the *three* most important words from both lists, and why?

2 Find these words in your dictionary.

arrest cast cell eagle lawyer weapon

Which of them go in these sentences?

a A prisoner sleeps in a . . . . . .
b My brother is a . . . . . .
c A(n) . . . . . is a dangerous bird.
d The police . . . . . him for carrying a . . . . . in the street.
e She has a . . . . . on her leg.

After you read

3 Look at these place names.

Boston Chicago Mill River New York
San Francisco San Jose

Which of them go in the following sentences?

a Spenser lives in . . . .
b He gets a letter from . . . .
c He flies to . . . ., then drives through . . . . to . . . .
d Spenser and Hawk find a safe place in . . . .
e A friend in . . . . gives Spenser information.
f Russell Costigan's wife lives in . . . .
g Spenser goes back to . . . . to get a car and some money.

4 Make correct sentences.

a Susan Silverman   is married to a dishonest man.
b Russell Costigan   is dead.
c Emmett Colder   is Spenser's friend.
d Jerry Costigan   has lost three teeth.
e Hawk   owns a weapons company.
f Tyler Smithson   can't decide between two men.

42

5 How are these important to the story?

    a lawyers   **b** the police   **c** Transpan

Chapters 5–7

Before you read

6 How will the Costigans feel when they learn that Hawk has escaped from prison? What will they do, do you think?

7 Find the word *train* in your dictionary. What is the difference between *train* and *teach*? Make sentences using each word.

8 What is the difference between the CIA and the FBI? Which one is connected with   **a** spies?   **b** catching criminals?

After you read

9 Choose the correct answer.

    a The FBI and CIA want

        (i) Russell Costigan to die.   (ii) to save Susan Silverman.

        (iii) Spenser and Hawk to do a job for them.

    b A man comes with Ives to the flat in Charleston. Spenser thinks he is

        (i) dangerous.   (ii) bad at his job.   (iii) useful.

    c Tyler Smithson stays with her husband because

        (i) he's rich.   (ii) he's good to be with.   (iii) she loves him.

    d Hawk and Spenser get jobs at the weapons factory because

        (i) they make friends with the workers.

        (ii) the CIA help them.

        (iii) they know a lot about weapons.

10 What do the underlined words mean?

    a 'Why did you do all those things?' (page 14)

    b 'That's against the law.' (page 17)

    c 'And if we do it . . . You'll get the California police to forget all about us?' (page 18)

    d 'He kicks them out of his house . . .' (page 22)

    e 'It's very safe.' (page 23)

11 Work with another student. Act out this conversation between Spenser and a man working for Costigan.

Student A: You work for Costigan. You see Spenser coming out of Tyler Smithson's flat. Ask him about his visit.

Student B: You are Spenser. Explain your visit.

Chapters 8 –11

Before you read

12 Why does Hawk want to speak to the Vietnamese workers, do you think? What do you think he will say?

13 Find these words in your dictionary.

alarm   mine   passage   roof-rack   van

Which of them can you

a see on top of a car? **c** hear? **e** work in

b drive? **d** walk along? underground?

After you read

14 Spenser says: 'It will be better for the Vietnamese to help us than to wait for Transpan to kick them out.' (page 30) Do you agree with him? Why, or why not?

15 How does Susan know that Spenser really loves her?

16 How does Russell Costigan help Spenser, and why?

Writing

17 You are a Mill River policeman. Write a report for your boss about Hawk's escape from prison.

18 You are a Vietnamese worker at the weapons factory. Describe an ordinary working day.

19 You are Tyler Smithson. You finally decide to leave Russell Costigan. Write him a letter, and explain why.

20 Write a description of Spenser. Is he a good man or a bad man, do you think? Say why.